THE ADVENTURES OF SUGAR AND JUNIOR

by Angela Shelf Medearis
illustrated by Nancy Poydar

Holiday House/New York

Text copyright © 1995 by Angela Shelf Medearis
Illustrations copyright © 1995 by Nancy Poydar
Printed in the United States of America
First Edition

Library of Congress Cataloging-in-Publication Data
Medearis, Angela Shelf, 1956–
      the adventures of Sugar and Junior / by Angela Shelf Medearis ;
   illustrated by Nancy Poydar. — 1st ed.
          p.   cm.
      Summary: Santiago Antonio Ramirez, also known as Junior, enjoys
   playing games, making cookies, and going to the movies with Sugar,
   the new girl next door.
      ISBN 0-8234-1182-6
      [1. Friendship — Fiction.   2. Hispanic Americans — Fiction.]
   I. Poydar, Nancy, ill.   II. Title.
   PZ7.M51274Ad   1995   94-42368   CIP   AC
   [Fic] — dc20

Contents

Chapter One/The New Neighbors

Junior Ramirez lived in Apartment 4A. A new family was moving into Apartment 4B. Junior watched them bring in box after box. There was a little girl near his age in the family. Junior was very excited. Now he had someone to play with.

"Hi!" he said.

"Hi!"

"My name is Junior. Do you want to play basketball?"

"Okay."

"We can play follow-the-leader while we walk to the park," said Junior.

"Fine, but let me be first," the girl said. She started to hop down the street.

Junior hopped after her. "What's your name?" he asked.

"My name is Sugar Johnson."

"But what's your *real* name?"

"That *is* my real name. What's yours?"

"Santiago Antonio Ramirez, Jr. Everybody calls me Junior for short. It's my nickname."

"Well," Sugar said, "Sugar is *not* my nickname."

"How did you get a name like Sugar?" Junior asked. He tried to turn a cartwheel, too. He fell over and landed on his back.

"What's the matter with my name?" asked Sugar. She started walking backwards.

"Nothing. But I have never met a girl with a name like that." Junior started walking backwards, too. He bumped into a big tree. "Ouch," he said. He rubbed his head. Then he followed Sugar into the playground.

Sugar began to climb the monkey bars. "Do you really want to know how I got my name?" she asked.

"Yes."

"My momma promised my aunt Sheila that she'd name me after her," Sugar said.

"Yo," said Junior, "I get it. So your real name is Sheila?"

9

"Part of it is," said Sugar. "My momma also promised my aunt Ursula that she'd name me after her."

"Your real name is Sheila Ursula?"

"Well, some of it is," said Sugar. "My momma made a mistake. She promised my aunt Georgia that she'd name me after her, too."

"So, your real name is Sheila Ursula Georgia Johnson?"

"No," said Sugar. "My aunt Anita also wanted me to be named after her."

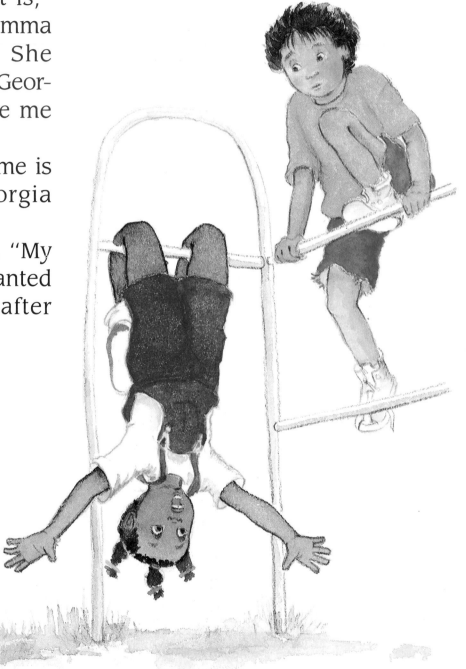

Sugar ran over to the swings and sat down. She swung higher and higher.

"Okay, okay!" said Junior. "Your name is Sheila Ursula Georgia Anita Johnson." He swung higher and higher, too.

"It was for a little while. Then my aunt Renée came to the hospital. She asked that I be named after her."

"Oh no! Your name is Sheila Ursula Georgia Anita Renée Johnson. Your momma gave you all those names?"

"No," Sugar said. "My daddy said those names were too many for one little baby."

Sugar jumped out of the swing. Then she ran to the basketball court.

"So what happened?" Junior asked as he ran after her.

"Well, my momma didn't want to hurt anyone's feelings. So, she decided to use one letter from each name.

S for Sheila,
U for Ursula,
G for Georgia,
A for Anita, and
R for Renée."

"Oh," said Junior. "That spells Sugar! I get it now!"

Sugar dribbled the ball. Then she threw it through the hoop.

"Two points," she said. "Now I will tell you my nickname."

"You have a nickname, too? What is it?"

Sugar made another basket. "Hoops," she said, "because I'm so good at basketball."

Chapter Two/The Cooks

One day Junior went to visit Sugar. She was in the kitchen. She was mixing something in a big bowl.

"What are you making, Sugar?" Junior asked.

"I'm making cookies," said Sugar.

"Can I help?"

"Sure. I need two eggs."

Junior looked in the refrigerator. "You only have one egg," he said.

"That's okay. I don't like eggs that much anyway."

Junior cracked the egg into the bowl. Pieces of eggshell fell into the bowl, too.

"I'll get them out," said Sugar. She tried and she tried, but she couldn't pick them out.

"Let me try," Junior said. But he couldn't pick them out, either.

"These will be real crunchy cookies," said Sugar.

"We need to put in some sugar," Junior suggested. "I like my cookies real sweet."

"I need two cups," said Sugar.

"You only have one cup," Junior answered.

"That will have to do," Sugar said.

"Let's put in some flour," suggested Junior. "That way, we'll have lots of cookies."

"Okay." Sugar dumped in four cups of flour. The flour made a big cloud of dust.

Junior began to cough. "Man," he said, "we're going to have a lot of cookies."

Sugar and Junior took turns stirring the cookie dough. Sugar rolled the dough into balls. Junior put them on the cookie sheets.

"It's four o'clock," Junior said. "I've got to go home now."

"Bye," said Sugar. "I'll bake the cookies tonight. Then I'll bring some to school tomorrow."

The next day, Sugar gave Junior a bag full of cookies. He took one and put the bag in his pocket.

"They look good," Junior said.
"Yes," said Sugar. "They do look good."
"They smell good."
"Yes. They smell real good."

Junior bit into one of the cookies. "These cookies taste horrible. Yuck! They're too hard."

"I know. I tried to eat one last night. I almost broke my front teeth," said Sugar.

"Oh well," Junior said. "I guess we're not very good cooks."

"No," Sugar said. "I guess not. Come on, it's time for art."

"Oh no. I forgot to bring a rock to paint for art."

"I forgot my rock, too," said Sugar. She looked sad.

"I have an idea," Junior said. He gave her one of the cookies. "These may be terrible cookies, but they will make wonderful rocks!"

Chapter Three/The Scary Movie

Sugar and Junior went to the movies. They paid for their tickets.

"I know all about this movie," Junior said. "My friend Ramón told me about it."

"Is it scary?" asked Sugar.

"It's real scary. But don't worry. I'll hold your hand."

"Does it have monsters in it?" asked Sugar.

"It has lots of monsters in it. But don't be scared, Sugar. I'll hold your hand."

They found seats close to the front.

"This movie is going to make you scream," said Junior.

Soon the movie started. It was scary. It had lots of monsters. Someone kept screaming and screaming.

It was Junior. He screamed every time he saw a monster.

"Junior," said Sugar, "please stop screaming. I can't hear."

Junior hid his face behind his hands. He hid behind the seats. He screamed and he screamed.

"Junior," said Sugar, "please stop screaming. The movie is over. Everyone has left but us."

"See?" said Junior as he crawled from under the seat. "I told you it was a scary movie."

"I think I like scary movies," said Sugar.

It was getting dark outside.

"Do you think there are scary monsters in the dark?" asked Junior.

"Yes," Sugar said, "but don't worry. I'll hold your hand, all the way home."

And she did.

Chapter Four/The Ice Cream Cone

It was hot! Sugar and Junior decided to buy some ice cream.

"I know what flavor I'm going to get," Sugar said.

"Which one?" asked Junior.

"Chocolate," said Sugar. "I love chocolate."

"I like chocolate, too."

"One scoop of chocolate, please," Sugar said.

"Cup or cone?" asked the ice cream man.

"On a cone." Sugar paid the ice cream man.

Junior looked at all the ice cream. He walked up and down.

"Cherry ice cream tastes good," suggested Sugar.

"I know. I had that kind last week."

"You could buy some vanilla," Sugar said.

"I don't want vanilla."

Finally Junior made up his mind. "Could I please taste the Rocky Road Munchy Crunchy Special?" he asked.

The ice cream man gave Junior a spoonful.

"Yuck," Junior said. "That tastes awful! I didn't know it had marshmallows in it."

"Oh Junior," said Sugar, "the Rocky Road Munchy Crunchy Special always has marshmallows in it."

"Why didn't you tell me?"

"You didn't ask."

Junior walked up and down. Up and down.

"Could I please taste the Very Berry Strawberry?" Junior asked.

The ice cream man gave Junior a spoonful.

"That tastes good," said Junior.

"Okay," said Sugar. "Get a scoop and let's go home."

"I said it tastes good," Junior said. "I didn't say I wanted to buy some."

"Oh man," said Sugar, "when are you going to
make up your mind?"
"I'll be ready in a minute," Junior said.

"Here," said Sugar, "hold my ice cream cone while I drink some water."

"Okay."

Sugar went to the water fountain. She was gone a long time. Her ice cream began to melt. Drip, drip, drip.

Junior took a bite of Sugar's ice cream. It was good. He took another bite. And another. And another.

Sugar came back from the water fountain.

"Junior," said Sugar. "Where is my ice cream?"

"I ate it."

"Junior!" said Sugar.

"It was melting. I'll buy you another cone."

"Okay."

Sugar looked at all the ice cream. She walked up and down.

"The Very Berry Strawberry tastes good," suggested Junior.

"I know," Sugar answered. "I had it last week."

"May I taste the Lemon Lime Sourball Special?" asked Sugar.

The ice cream man gave Sugar a spoonful.

"That tastes good," said Sugar.

"Okay," said Junior. "I'll pay for it."

"I said it tastes good," Sugar said. "I didn't say I wanted some."

"Oh man," said Junior. "Come on! It's time to go home."

"I just can't seem to make up my mind."

"How about some chocolate?" asked Junior.

"That's a great idea," Sugar said. "But let's get two scoops this time. One for you and one for me."